All You Need is Love

Emma Chichester Clark

JONATHAN CAPE
LONDON

For all my friends in the park —
Rocket, Esther, Bean, Jakey,
and Tosca — and my sister Liffey.

Emma Chichester Clark began the website **Plumdog Blog** in 2012, chronicling the real-life adventures
of her lovable "whoosell" (whippet, Jack Russell and poodle cross) Plum. Emma soon gained thousands
of loyal Plumdog devotees, and in 2014 a book of the blog was published by Jonathan Cape.
This picture book story is the third Plumdog book for children.

JONATHAN CAPE

UK I USA I Canada I Ireland I Australia
India I New Zealand I South Africa

Jonathan Cape is part of the Penguin Random House group of companies
whose addresses can be found at global.penguinrandomhouse.com.

www.penguin.co.uk   www.puffin.co.uk   www.ladybird.co.uk

Penguin
Random House
UK

First published 2019
001

Printed in China
A CIP catalogue record for this book is available from the British Library

ISBN: 978-0-857-55199-3

All correspondence to:
Jonathan Cape, Penguin Random House Children's
80 Strand, London WC2R ORL

MIX
Paper from
responsible sources
FSC
www.fsc.org   FSC® C018179

I AM PLUM!
And I love everyone!

Well, **NEARLY** everyone . . .

I love my mummy,
Emma,

and my daddy,
Rupert,

and Binky the cat,

and Sam and Gracie
who live next door.

And I love my friends

Rocket,

Esther,

Bean

and Jakey.

We love chasing each other around the park!

We are **absolutely** best friends and the best chasers in the world!

But today there
was a new dog.

"Say hello to
Milly," said Rocket.
"She'd like to
play with us."

But I thought Milly looked very small — and **very** silly.

She didn't look like she'd be much good at chasing.

And we didn't **need** a silly little Milly.

So, I decided to ignore her.

I pretended I simply couldn't see her.

Eventually, she gave up and went away.

"Now we can play!"
I told my friends.

"I'm surprised at you!"
said Esther.

And she didn't mean
it in a good way.

Just then, an old dog with a scary face turned up.

"That's Bounder!" said Jakey. "He's our new friend."

I definitely didn't want to be chased by Bounder.

"We don't need a new friend," I said.

So, I told him. "We don't need you."

I gave him my fiercest look,

and then I chased him away!

I hoped my friends would see how brave I was.

"Now can we play?" I asked them.

But they weren't even listening to me.

They were running around with a dog that was as big as a horse!

"It's Otto!" cried Rocket.

They all seemed very pleased to see him.

But I could see he was far too big for chasing and I definitely, definitely didn't want him to chase me.

So, I barked at him fiercely.

I said he COULD NOT play with US.

He looked really scared.

He shivered and
trembled and
hurried away.

"Now it's only
us again!" I said.
"LET'S PLAY!"

But my friends
just looked
at me.

"Not with you, Plum," said Esther.

"No, you're far too mean," said Bean.

Even Emma seemed to be upset with me. She marched me home early.

She told my daddy
all about it.

"I was so
disappointed
in Plum today,"
she said.

"Oh, Plum,"
said my daddy.
"How would you
feel if someone
did that to you?"

"Everyone needs love," said Gracie.

"Whether they're big or they're small," said Sam.
"Or hairy or scary," said Gracie.

Even Otto? I wondered.
Or Bounder, or Milly?

It was a few days before I was allowed back in the park, and I couldn't wait to see my friends again. I was sure they must be missing me as much as I'd missed them.

But none of them came to say hello.
They were busy playing with their new friends.
Maybe they were happier without me . . .

I felt so left out. It was a **terrible** feeling. And that's when I realised - Milly, Bounder and even Otto - I'd made **them** feel like this, too.

I needed to say sorry.

First, I said
sorry to Milly.

And then I said
sorry to Bounder.

And then I said
sorry to Otto.

"Well done, Plum!"
said Esther.

"Brilliant,"
said Rocket.

And, do you know? The whole day changed.
It was **BRILLIANT**, just like Rocket said.

EVERYONE chased EVERYONE brilliantly.
We were all friends now.

"I'm proud of you, Plum," said Emma.

Sam said, "Me too!"
"Because all you need is love,
whether you're big or you're small," said Gracie.
"It's true, Plum," said Emma. "Or hairy and scary
. . . **LIKE YOU!**"